The
Sea Man

The Sea Man

JANE YOLEN

Illustrations by

CHRISTOPHER DENISE

Philomel Books   New York

Text copyright © 1997 by Jane Yolen
Illustrations copyright © 1997 by Christopher Denise
All rights reserved. This book, or parts thereof, may not be reproduced
in any form without permission in writing from the publisher,
Philomel Books, 200 Madison Avenue, New York, NY 10016.
Philomel Books Reg. U.S. Pat. & Tm Off.
Published simultaneously in Canada. Printed in The United States.
Book design by Patrick Collins and Donna Mark. The text is set in Bembo.

Library of Congress Cataloging-in-Publication Data
Yolen, Jane.   The sea man / Jane Yolen;
with illustrations by Christopher Denise.   p.   cm.
Summary: When sailors aboard a Dutch ship in 1663 capture a creature,
half man and half fish, the superstitious crewmen want to kill it,
except for a young cabin boy who believes that the creature deserves to live.
[1. Mermen—Fiction. 2. Netherlands—Fiction.]   I. Denise, Christopher, ill.
II. Title PZ7.Y78Sb 1997   [Fic]—dc20   95-52051 CIP AC
ISBN 0-399-22939-6 (hardcover)

10   9   8   7   6   5   4   3   2   1   First Impression

For Betsy Pucci Stemple,
who has her own magic.

THE SKY OVER the sea is a deep blue slate.

"And neither bird nor cloud dares write upon it, my darling daughter, Jannie," Lieutenant Huiskemp writes in his careful script. "But there are always wonders below the water. Not magic, dear one. Just things we do not know yet. But once seen and examined, these wonders can be explained."

He draws tiny dolphins and flying fish in the margins of his letter. They leap from line to line, a strange punctuation. "I send you kisses, safe and snug in Zeeland. And kisses, too, for your dear mama. You must be a good girl and not cry when she combs your hair or complain over much when she plaits it. Your loving father, Maarten Huiskemp, April 1663."

He looks out across the water to the shore. There the mills spin the heavy wind in their long arms. Cattle graze the dike grasses. Along the roadside, thousands of colored tulips bow and bend with every passing breeze.

Lieutenant Huiskemp smiles, stands, and stretches. The wind puzzles through his yellow hair. He is a tall man, his legs like a stork's, long and bony. He towers above the men in his crew. When he sits down again, he draws a whale at the bottom of the letter spouting Jannie's name. Then he draws a portrait of Jannie herself, brown braids standing out stiff to each side. He adds a fish tail instead of legs, so that she looks as if she is swimming next to the whale.

Though he does not believe mermaids are real, never having seen any, the lieutenant knows Jannie will like the pictures. She loves the fairy stories he reads to her and soon enough she will have to give up such childish things. Besides, it is the last letter he can send her for a long time. Presently his ship, *The Water Nix,* bobbing at anchor off the coast, must join the fleet in the open sea.

There is a sound behind him and the lieutenant turns quickly. It is the young cabin boy, Pieter, just newly come aboard. He has yet to learn their quiet ways.

"Do you want some tea, sir?" Pieter asks. His voice still holds the word in awe, for tea is something only the captain and the lieutenant are allowed, it being a rare and expensive drink.

"No, son," Lieutenant Huiskemp says. "But you can tell me what you think of this." He holds the letter up. The breeze makes it ripple like the sea.

"I cannot read it, sir," Pieter says, brushing the fair hair from his eyes.

The lieutenant catches hold of the end and pulls the letter tight against the wind.

"I mean, I cannot read, sir," Pieter says. There is fresh color in his cheeks.

"Neither can my little girl, Jannie," the lieutenant says quickly. "That is why I draw pictures for her. Surely . . ." He chuckles, and it is a comforting sound. "Surely you can read them."

Pieter smiles shyly. "I can read pictures, sir." Leaning over to look at the letter, his hands carefully behind him, he says: "Why, it is a sperm whale, I think, sir. And a *zee wyven,* a mermaid, there at the bottom. My father saw one once."

"A whale?" the lieutenant asks.

"A mermaid," Pieter says seriously.

"Did he?" The lieutenant keeps a straight face. He will not laugh at Pieter. He respects all his men, and this one is young enough to learn the difference between science and stories. But not, the lieutenant feels, by means of laughter.

"He saw it at a fair," Pieter answers.

"Do not believe everything you see at a fair," the lieutenant says, matching Pieter in seriousness. "Sometimes it is nothing more than a trick of mirrors and smoke that men play to steal your coins. Or a monkey's head sewn to the tail of a carp. To fool the gullible."

"I will remember that, sir," Pieter says. But he does not sound quite convinced.

"Good boy." Lieutenant Huiskemp dismisses Pieter with a nod and bends back to his letter. This time he writes to his wife, but there are no fancies in it. It is about the weather and the waywardness of man.

CHAPTER

2

THE SKY HAS NOT CHANGED the whole of the day. Except for birds scripting across its empty slate, the sky is the same.

On board *The Water Nix* it has been a day of preparations. The busy sailors scrub and rub and polish the ship, getting it ready for its voyage out to the open sea. By early evening, the sky has darkened overhead, but otherwise has not changed.

Lieutenant Huiskemp is once again on deck. This time Pieter is more quiet in his approach, but still the lieutenant hears him. He turns and looks sternly at the boy, setting down the spyglass with which he has been checking the shore.

"Do you want something to eat, sir?" Pieter asks.

Just as the lieutenant is about to answer, there is a shout from one of the sailors. It shatters the peace of the ship.

"Look! Look!"

Huiskemp shades his eyes against the sun so low on the horizon. He walks on his stork legs to the other side of the ship. Pieter follows behind, like a shadow.

The men are boiling around the railing, jostling one another. They are pointing out to the open sea.

The lieutenant sees an odd whirling in the water, as if it were pleated like a piece of cloth. He has never seen anything like it before. "What is going on?" he asks.

"Something horrible!" shouts one of the sailors, his eyes never leaving the troubled waters.

The lieutenant is not one for fast judgments, though he is one for quick actions. With his spyglass he watches where the water is roiling.

Suddenly a hand rises out of the water, then an arm, two arms, a man's head. It looks as if the man is praying or shouting for help, but oddly he makes no sound.

"Sir, he is drowning," Pieter cries.

"Lower a boat at once," the lieutenant commands. He does not take the spyglass from his eye.

A sailor named Henk and two others, Hans and Wilhelm, are lowered in the rescue boat and they row over the troubled sea. Along the railing, the other sailors call out instructions. Only the lieutenant and Pieter are silent, the one because he knows the men and trusts them; the other, who is too new for trust, because he does not.

The strange pleated waves never trouble *The Water Nix,* but they do rock the little rescue boat, so much that Hans and Wilhelm must hold on to the sides to keep from falling out. Only Henk, his hands on the oars, seems oblivious to the motion. The muscles on his arms bunch and pleat much like the sea as he rows.

When the rescue boat reaches the man, Wilhelm frantically signals back to the ship. Hans shouts something, but it is carried away by the wind. They bend over the side and struggle to lift the man into the boat.

The lieutenant can see he is tangled in netting. He has broad, muscular shoulders and dark curly hair glinting green, like phosphorescence.

"Like a Portugee," whispers Pieter.

The lieutenant glares at him and Pieter is suddenly

silenced, recalling that he has been lectured before about saying such things.

When the man is halfway into the boat, everyone can see that he is not entirely a man! From the waist up he is as human as the sailors. But below the waist, he is a fish, with a tail like a tunny's, the scales all silver and blue and the water beading off them like jewels.

The lieutenant lowers his spyglass, but even without it he can see the tail. Still he will not let himself believe.

In the boat, Hans and Wilhelm try to push the creature back into the water. Henk takes one oar from the oarlock, prepared to beat the sea man into submission.

Recalled to his duty, Lieutenant Huiskemp picks up a speaking trumpet and shouts through it. "Bring that . . . thing . . . on board. Bring it on board." He is quite suddenly excited. And he is puzzled. *It is a mystery,* he reminds himself. *And once examined . . .*

Being good sailors, Henk and Hans and Wilhelm obey, though first they wrap the sea man more securely in the net. Then, staying as far away from the creature as they dare, they row it back to the ship.

"But why, sir?" asks young Pieter. "Why bring the thing on board?"

The question is one the lieutenant asks himself as quickly, so he does not reprimand the boy for asking. But he mumbles out the only answer he can find. "In the interests of science, lad. The captain will want to have a look at it when he returns." He adds to himself in sober contemplation, *As do I. As do I.*

CHAPTER

3

THE SLATE OF SKY is a strange orange and gray now, orange from the setting sun, gray around the edges, as night creeps in.

When the sea man is drawn up on the deck, tangled in netting, the sailors crowd around for a good look. Up close, the sea man looks more and more like a fish. There are webbings as gray as storm air between its fingers. Its mouth is round like a fish's; its eyes a pale, watery blue. There are gray-green hairs curling on its chest in the pattern of seashells. It has red gill slits along its neck. It lies gray and gasping on the deck and does not speak.

"What a hideous thing," says Hans. He looks at the sea man from the safety of nearly five feet away. Having touched it once, he does not want to have to do so again.

The sea man suddenly slaps its tail against the deck and all the men jump back. The sound is as loud as a cannon shot.

"That is bad luck," Henk says, smoothing his fair mustache. "We should kill it."

"We should sell it," says Wilhelm. The others agree. They argue about prices while the sea man gasps.

"Sell it?" asks Pieter. "Sell it where? To a fair? My father saw a *zee wyven* once at a fair. But it was much smaller, he said. About the size of a carp."

"Sell it to the university professors in Leyden," says Wilhelm. "They would give many guilders to study it."

Slap. Slap. The tail against the deck is not so loud now.

"Bad luck," Henk repeats. He spits in the sea man's direction.

"University professors do not care about luck," says Wilhelm.

Henk spits again. "All men care about luck."

The sea man wriggles along the deck but still makes no sound, except for the *slap-slap* of its tail. Its round mouth opens and closes soundlessly.

The lieutenant is equally silent. For a moment he feels as if he is drowning in a dream.

Henk leans over. "Phew. And it smells."

Another sailor laughs, but not heartily. "Like a fish."

Wilhelm slaps his thigh. "Like a Portu—"

The lieutenant opens his mouth, interrupts. "What would you have it smell like? It *is* a fish. It only looks, in this light, like a man."

"Such things are bad luck," Henk repeats. "We should kill it quickly and *then* sell it to the professors. They will not care if it is alive or dead. It is bad luck, I tell you. I felt it when I put my hand on its back. The bad luck came right through my fingers." He holds up his right hand as if the print of the luck might be seen. His other hand reaches for the knife at his belt.

"No knives, man," the lieutenant says, "or I will put you in irons in the hold."

All this time the sea man has been silent, though its mouth opens and closes, opens and closes.

"Is it deaf, sir?" asks Pieter, talking to the lieutenant. "I have an uncle in Haarlem who is deaf. He does not make a sound, either." Without waiting for an answer, the boy kneels down by the sea man and puts his hand on the creature's shoulder. He shouts into its shell-like ear. He seems absolutely unafraid, as if his youth confers on him some kind of immortality. "Are you deaf?"

At the shout, the sea man's eyes open wide. Its head jerks back. Its arms, still bound to its side by the netting, move as much as they can. The right hand is partially clear of the net, and the fingers wriggle slightly; the webbing between wobbles.

Pieter turns his head and looks at the lieutenant, his hand still on the creature's bare gray shoulder. "Not deaf, then, sir." He stands up and moves back, away from the sea man who is once again still. Pieter does not, even once, wipe his hand on his shirt.

The sailors break their tight circle around the sea man and look somewhat ashamed, all except Henk, whose face has grown dark, like the sky.

"About your work, men," says the lieutenant. And they go, though they still manage to keep an eye on the creature. The lieutenant, however, kneels down beside it. He speaks to it in Dutch, then Danish, German, and English. He speaks slowly, as if to a child or to a simpleton. He tries French. At last he says a few words in Portuguese.

The sea man opens its mouth again. This close, the lieutenant can see that its mouth is hollow. Like a fish, it has teeth, but no tongue. "Of course you cannot talk," the lieutenant murmurs. Only Pieter—and the sea man—hear him.

At the lieutenant's voice, this time the sea man tries to sit up.

"Who are you?" the lieutenant asks in Dutch. *"What are you?"* he asks, even more slowly. He points at the sea man when he says this and draws a question mark between them with his finger.

The sea man sits all the way up, watching the lieutenant's fingers with its watery eyes. Some of the netting is draped over its hunched shoulders like a shawl, so it looks like an old man. A gray old man. The fingers on its one free hand wave quickly, like seaweed in a heavy swell. *Like a semaphore,* the lieutenant thinks. It is not a comfortable thought.

"Careful," Henk calls from his place far back on the deck. Even in the quickening dark, he has seen the movement. "It is dangerous. Surely its bite is full of poison."

"Give me your knife," the lieutenant says at last, holding out his hand. "Quickly, man."

Henk runs forward and hands him the knife. "Fillet it," he says. "It will make a big stew."

CHAPTER

4

A SOLITARY GULL writes a warning on the sky slate, then
dives down into the sea. No one sees it. They are all
intent on the knife in the lieutenant's hand. They are
as silent as the sea man.

Lieutenant Huiskemp slices through the netting, entirely freeing the sea man's hands and forearms. The sea
man flexes its left fingers, then the right, and the sailors
freeze for a moment, as if the flexing fingers have en-
chanted them.

Suddenly the sea man makes rapid, strange signs with
both its hands, right and left crossing in complicated pat-
terns. The webbings between the fingers pulse green
and pink and gray. Then the right hand reaches for the
lieutenant's knife.

Grabbing his own knife, Wilhelm lurches forward. "Look out!" he cries. And adds as an afterthought, "Sir!"

"Stop, man!" The lieutenant holds up the hand with the knife, stopping Wilhelm in his tracks. With his other hand, the lieutenant takes hold of the sea man's fingers. They are slippery and wet and cold. They tap out some kind of message in the lieutenant's palm, but though the lieutenant knows many languages, this is not one of them. *Still,* he thinks, *only humans have language.*

He drops the creature's hand and turns to the men. "A fish is not dangerous out of the water. Come, help me with this thing. . . ."

The sailors look at him strangely. One even crosses himself. The others back away.

"Touch it again, sir?" Henk asks. "We are not crazy. Not like the boy."

Lieutenant Huiskemp says, "Captain Van Tassel will be back tonight with our orders. He will want to see this creature alive. Until then, we will keep it safe in the hold." He puts a hand on Pieter's shoulder and says to the men, "Only this boy has shown any real courage."

At that the men grumble, and Hans reminds them all

that he and Wilhelm and Henk have already done their share. So three others, mouths set in a way to indicate they have found their own courage, pick up the sea man; but their eyes, frightened, give them away. They carry the creature—one by the shoulders, two at the tail—to the hold door, which Henk pulls open. There they heave the sea man once, twice, and throw it in.

It lands with a loud *thunk* and, after a moment, they hear another noise. The creature is whistling. The sound is soft and mournful.

"A sea song?" Hans asks.

"A dirge," the lieutenant whispers. He knows that whales can sing. And wolves. He knows that birds can whistle. "A dirge."

Only young Pieter hears him.

CHAPTER

5

THE SKY'S SLATE is now a soft night blue. Only one star is out, like punctuation to a sentence yet to be written.

In his cabin, the lieutenant has eaten dinner alone and thinks about the sea man. Since he has seen it, since he has touched it, he must believe it is real. A sea man in the flesh, not in the imagination.

"But a sea man is not really a man," he tells himself. He sets out his argument carefully. "It is a creature of the ocean, of the deep. An animal. A fish. We have not yet explored all that is below. This creature is a mystery. But it is not magic. Science will, in the end, explain all." Still, he is uncomfortable with his reasoning and does not know why, so he turns his thoughts to the sea man in the hold. He wonders how long it can live there, away from the ministrations of the sea.

He stands and paces his cabin once, then twice. *A fish,* he reminds himself, *dies out of the water.* He is decided. He will check on it and, in the interests of science, give it what it needs.

The men on the deck are clustered about the forecastle, talking in whispers. The lieutenant says nothing to them but goes directly to the dark hold. He lights a lantern, raises it high. The sea man looks up at the light with clouded eyes. It waves a feeble hand.

Leaving the light, the lieutenant goes up on deck, fills a bucket with seawater, and carries it down again. Even when he douses the sea man with the water, the creature scarcely moves.

For a moment, a long moment, they stare at each other in silence. There is something compelling about the creature, mesmerizing, but not evil. *Henk is wrong about that.*

"Are you . . ." the lieutenant begins. "Do you . . ." Then he stops entirely and shakes his head. "You are a creature," he says. "And understand no more than my wife's dog, Tulip."

The sea man makes no answer.

Taking the lantern with him, Lieutenant Huiskemp goes up the stairs once more. The air above is suddenly cool and fresh smelling. He breathes it in gratefully, then sighs.

Young Pieter is standing at the railing, looking out across the dark ocean. The sky is now fully lit by a round moon and flickering stars.

"The captain did not come back with the evening tide," Pieter says.

"Then he will come in the morning," the lieutenant answers. He is not sure the creature will be alive then, but he does not say this to Pieter.

"Sir, Henk is telling stories about sea dragons and kraken and the vengeance of the mer," Pieter says. His voice trembles and he sounds, suddenly, very young. A child. "He says they are all evil. That they are satanic. That they have no souls."

The lieutenant nods solemnly. He can hear Henk's voice now, coming through the breezeless dark. Henk is a strong storyteller and the sea makes believers of all men. Lieutenant Huiskemp worries about the dying creature in the hold; about Henk, who is rousing the sailors; about the trembling boy at his side.

"So you believe so, sir?" Pieter asks.

The lieutenant startles, then turns his head toward the boy. "Believe what, son?"

"That the sea man has no soul."

"It is one of God's own creatures," he says slowly. "And as such, we must love it. But the only one with a soul, so Scripture tells us, is man. It is what distinguishes us from animals." He pauses. "And from fish." He does not tell Pieter that it is *language* that truly distinguishes humankind from the lower orders. Science and religion are too heady a mix for this unlettered boy.

"But what of the story of the water nix, sir?" Pieter asks.

"The story of our boat?" For a moment the lieutenant is confused.

"No," Pieter says. "It is an old tale my father told me. He said there was once a priest who met a water nix who begged and begged him to baptize her. But he refused, saying that as she was a water sprite, she had no soul. He told her, 'Sooner would my old walking stick sprout leaves than a nix shall have a soul.' And even as he spoke, green furled from the stick: stems and vines and leaves." Pieter takes a deep breath. "Is that true, sir? I mean, how could it be, if what Henk says is true?"

"It is a story," the lieutenant says.

"But is it *true?*" The boy asks, the tremor back in his voice.

The lieutenant is about to say *What is truth?* when the boy grabs his sleeve.

"Sir—look!" He points to the water. In the moon's light, the boy's hair is silvery and hardly seems real. "There is something in the water."

"There are dolphins," Lieutenant Huiskemp says, suddenly tired of the whole thing; of the distinction between what is real and what is true. He wishes to be far away, either at sea or on the shore. *In between,* he realizes, *is the most difficult of all places to be.* Like being a lieutenant but not captain; like being on board ship; like being a boy among men; like being a lettered man with an unlettered crew.

"There are whales," he adds. But still he looks to where Pieter is pointing and sees that there is, indeed, something odd there, though he cannot see it clearly. "Night," he says to the boy, "makes many things seem unnatural." But the tremor is now in his own voice.

Pieter turns to him and, in a voice made old by truth, declares, "There is a sea man in our hold and we pulled it in by day. You told me such things were tricks to get coins. Yet there he is, half man and half fish."

Half man and half fish, the lieutenant thinks. *Someone else who is in between.* He speaks quickly, as if truth can be made by running words together. "What is in the hold is a fish, not a man." He wishes he could believe that entirely. Or believe otherwise. "And it is dying out of the sea."

"Dying?" There is a world of sorrow in the boy's one word. It shames Huiskemp to his very soul. Then the boy grabs his sleeve once more. "Sir—that *something* in the sea. It is nearer still."

The lieutenant is forced to look more closely by his fear, by his hope, by the truth.

The sea, below the slate of sky, is strangely pleated once again.

6

THE SENTENCES WRITTEN on the night's slate are these:
full moon, a thousand stars, and the thinnest wisp of a
cloud, like a hyphen, against the moon. Something
dark and light is reflected in the sea.

"Quick, my boy," whispers the lieutenant, suddenly
decided, "you and I will haul that creature on deck. Soul
or no soul, perhaps this time it will speak to us in a way
we can understand. Perhaps it can tell us what is down
there, swimming by our ship's bow. Perhaps it knows if
that thing down there means us any harm. I am in charge
while the captain is away and I must guard the ship."

"What of the men, sir? Shouldn't they help?"

"They are captives of Henk's story, lad. At night a
tale has more command than any officer."

"I understand, sir," Pieter says. And the lieutenant is sure he does.

They hurry below. The smell in the hold is stronger now. It is a dark smell, and damp. It is redolent of decay. When Pieter lights the lantern, they see the sea man humped in a corner. It flings one green-gray arm across its eyes to shield them from the light, except it moves in slow motion, as if swimming. Its breath is labored, its gill slits now all gray.

"I will take the shoulders," says the lieutenant. "You carry the tail. We will move it to the stern, away from Henk and his stories."

They struggle with the sea man, who lies limp and heavy in their arms. Its skin is no longer slippery, no longer wet, but feels spongy and warm. Twice Pieter drops the tail on the stairs and it slaps against the steps, a loud thudding. The lieutenant breathes his worry through his teeth, a soft, nervous whistle. At the sound, the sea man tries to twist in the lieutenant's arms. It manages to look up in his face, but they are so far from the lantern's light, they are just two shadows in the dark. And in the dark, their faces are the same.

At last the lieutenant and Pieter wrestle the sea man onto the deck, near the starboard railing. They set it down and it breathes deeply for several long moments, as if gathering strength from the salt air. Then, hardly moving, it purses its lips and sends out a strange, frothy whistle. For a long while everything seems to still: the rocking ship, the hearty wind, the rolling waves, the sound of Henk's voice from the forecastle.

Then there is a sudden answer from the sea: a long, high, full whistle, ornamented with sweet flutings.

The sea man sits up. It begins to thrash and twist, humping and thumping against the railing. As it moves, its tired, dying whistle gains energy, changing to a stretched sad note, as loud and lowing as a foghorn.

The water below the boat grows more pleated still and *The Water Nix* bobs frantically at anchor. Henk's startled voice cries out in the dark. The other men echo him, like leader and chorus of a badly sung song.

Pieter and the lieutenant lean over the railing and stare at the pleated sea. Below them in the water is a figure outlined in moonlight. It has long, green curling hair. It has softly rounded breasts. It has a child in its arms. The child has a tail like an upside-down question mark and two green braids standing stiffly to either side.

"Lieutenant—look! A *zee wyven,*" says Pieter.

"A sea wife," the lieutenant whispers, staring. "She

has braided her daughter's hair." His voice is as awed as Pieter's, and by this one simple fact. "She has plaited it into two braids." At last he is a believer, science and story coming together.

At the sound of their voices, the child turns in her mother's arms. She puts her head back and the moon lights her face fully. She is laughing, but silently. Her little tail strokes the water. The sea wife's face shows no such delight. Drops of water—*Tears?* the lieutenant wonders—cascade down her cheeks.

Without a word, Lieutenant Huiskemp kneels by the sea man's side. Using his bare hands, he rips away the last of the netting from the sea man's shoulders, though he rips his own skin in the process. The blood drops, black, onto the sea man's skin. He seems to feel it and looks, briefly, into the lieutenant's eyes.

Huiskemp picks up the sea man and, staggering under the weight, hoists him upright against the railing.

"This is for my own little Jannie," he says. "And for the nix." He does not know himself if he means Pieter's story or the ship.

Pieter stoops down and, silently, gathers up the sea man's tail.

Just then, Henk and the other men move toward

them. Henk's knife is drawn and glitters cruelly in the moon's light.

"That thing is evil," Henk says. "If it goes back into the sea, it will raise a storm against us. All the old tales say so."

His arms filled with the fish-smelling sea man, the lieutenant cannot fight Henk with anything but the authority of his voice. He raises it against the wind, against the sound of the waves. "This is a man of the sea even as you are a man of the land," he says. "He has a language. He has a wife. He has a child."

"He has a tail," Henk mutters, and strikes with the knife. But Pieter has dropped the tail and runs between Henk and the sea man. The knife cuts Pieter on the arm and he cries out in pain. It is a cry that recalls them all to action. The men, who have stood by Henk all day, suddenly grab his knife arm and take the blade from him.

Lieutenant Huiskemp hoists the sea man over the rail. The sea man arches his back and flips over three times before knifing into the water in a perfect dive. When he surfaces again, he salutes the ship, then arrows back into the deep. His wife and child follow.

The pleated water stills. The boat ceases rocking.

There is a long silence, broken only by the sound of the waves against the hull. The men all stare at the quieted sea, Pieter holding his arm. It aches, but not more than his heart at the sea man's going.

"Well," Wilhelm says at last, "there is one curiosity the professors will not get to study."

"Nor will we see any money," says Hans.

"Mark me, he will send evil," Henk says. But no one listens to him.

Lieutenant Huiskemp smiles. "We will not see the sea man again." He turns and gestures with his right hand. The bleeding has stopped. "This deck is a great mess. I want it shipshape before Captain Van Tassel returns on the morning tide."

And as it is no more than an ordinary command, the sailors thankfully move to their tasks.

CHAPTER
7

BUT THE LIEUTENANT is wrong. When they set sail, for three nights running, under a clean slate of sky, the sea man surfaces again, surrounded by pleated water. He does not whistle, but his hands move quick and slow, quick and slow.

The lieutenant, who learns languages easily, learns to read those fingers. And he learns to speak the same way.

The first night the lieutenant picks up counting and grammar. He learns greetings, and the names of many things: water, fish, ship, bird, sky. The sea man teaches him the seven ways of describing waves and the thirteen terms for whale. There are separate names for *"zee wyven"* and "land wife," but the lieutenant is surprised to find that the word for "child" is the same.

The second night the two men exchange bits of history, which, like most family stories, are made up of equal parts of truth and of lies. On that second eve, the lieutenant speaks of life aboard ship, of the unlettered men who can still read their routes in the writing of the stars. His slow fingers tell the sea man how he, a Haarlem lad, trained to science and mathematics, came by slow, sure steps to the sea. His fingers stumble, trying to find words for "science" and "mathematics." The sea man, of course, has none. At last the lieutenant settles on gestures that show something being built up, bigger and bigger. Perhaps "creation" is what he has signed. Then he gestures finger added to finger, for "counting." The sea man seems to understand.

On the second night, they also speak of their homes. Huiskemp's hands talk of his Portuguese wife and his own dark-haired daughter, so like the sea man's own child. He outlines Jannie's braids against his own head, threading his fingers till they both laugh at the tangles. The lieutenant laughs out loud, a hearty sound, and the sea man laughs silently, his mouth full of bubbles. When the lieutenant is done, his hands ache, as one's ears ache after a long night of conversation with a friend.

But on the third night out at sea, the sea man does

not come with stories. He comes instead with a warning. He rises, whistling for attention, and then, hands and fingers frantic, he spells out wild waves, lightning, storms.

Patiently, the lieutenant translates for Captain Van Tassel and the crew. Even Henk is convinced. The captain orders them back to harbor, where they ride out the storm.

"And it was only the sea man's warnings," the lieutenant writes to Jannie at the bottom of the page, "that brought us safe to our mooring in view of the waving tulips and the windmills with the storms in their long arms. Only our ship was undamaged when so many others were battered and broken or lost at sea."

He decorates the envelope with a picture of the sea man and the sea wife and their little sea girl, who—except for the gray webbings between her fingers, except for the question-mark tail—looks remarkably like little Jannie Huiskemp, so safe upon the shore in a snug little home in Zeeland.

AUTHOR'S NOTE

WHEN DOING RESEARCH for a book on mermen, I came upon an understated paragraph: "In 1663 in Holland, sworn testimony was obtained from sailors who had 'captured a merman.' He was swimming, they said, off the Dutch coast and was caught by a lieutenant in the navy."

Who could resist such a note? And it is not the only report of such sightings and captures. In 1726, a Dutch colonial chaplain wrote a treatise called *A Natural History of Amboina,* in which he cites *zee menschen* (sea men) and *zee wyven* under the category of fish.

DATE DUE

NOV 3 0 1998	
DEC 1 1 1998	
JAN 0 5 1999	
MAY 2 2 1999	

BRODART, CO.   Cat. No. 23-221-003